PARARESCUE CORPS

BY MICHAEL P. SPRADLIN
ILLUSTRATED BY SPIROS KARKAVELAS

STONE ARCH BOOKS
a capstone imprint

VIPER STRIKE

A 4D BOOK

Pararescue Corps is published by
Stone Arch Books, A Capstone Imprint
1710 Roe Crest Drive
North Mankato, Minnesota 56003
www.mycapstone.com

Library of Congress Cataloging-in-Publication Data
is available on the Library of Congress website.
ISBN: 978-1-4965-5202-0 (Library Binding)
ISBN: 978-1-4965-5206-8 (eBookPDF)

Editor: Hank Musolf
Designer: Ted Williams
Production: Laura Manthe

Design Elements:

Shutterstock: John T Takai, MicroOne

Printed and bound in Canada.
PA020

Download the Capstone app!

- Ask an adult to download the Capstone 4D app.

- Scan the cover and stars inside the book for additional content.

When you scan a spread, you'll find
fun extra stuff to go with this book!
You can also find these things
on the web at www.capstone4D.com
using the password: strike.52020

TABLE OF CONTENTS

His name was Miguel Ramos. But he was known as *La Vibora*—the Viper. He lived in the tree-covered mountains of Venezuela. His camp was a collection of small cabins and tents. It was encircled by a tall fence. Propane generators provided power to the camp. There was a small garden and several vehicles inside the compound.

Through a clearing where he stood, he saw the capital city far below.

It was a place he could no longer go. He was a wanted man. An outlaw. But he considered himself a patriot. He was trying to save the Venezuelan people from a corrupt government, with officials who lie, cheat, and steal. Many followers in his camp believed in his cause. He called them the Army of Venom.

The city below was in chaos. People rioted in the streets. There was little food, and worse, no one had any money to buy it. Venezuela was one of the most oil-rich countries in the world. But the price of oil had dropped. Government corruption was so deep, it sold the oil and crooked politicians kept the money.

Despite rallies and demonstrations, Miguel failed to effect change. It was time for more desperate measures. It was time to strike a blow for freedom.

"Excuse me, señor," a voice behind him said.

"Yes Jorge?"

"She asks for you, señor. She is . . . she asks for you," he muttered.

"Thank you, Jorge," he said.

Miguel left his spot in the clearing and walked to one of the larger buildings in the compound. Inside it was cool. The generators hummed. He used a great deal of power for air conditioning to keep her comfortable. At her bedside, he placed a cool hand on her forehead. It was hot to the touch. The fever was still with her. She opened her eyes.

"My son," she said.

"*Madre*," he said, "how are you feeling?"

Miguel's mother reclined on the bed. Pillows

propped up her head and shoulders. She was so small that the bed seemed to swallow her up. Her white hair blended in with the pillow.

"Better," she said, coughing.

Miguel knew she was lying. She was so frail. She was not feeling better at all. She grew sicker by the day. He feared there was not much time left.

A bowl of water sat on a table next to her bed. He dipped a cloth into it and wiped her forehead. He carefully and gently washed her cheeks and lips. She licked at the moist cloth.

"Are you thirsty, Madre?" Miguel said.

Not waiting for an answer, he held a straw to her mouth. She drank deeply from the glass. Even these small efforts appeared to exhaust her. She sank back into the pillows.

"Miguel, my son?" she said.

"Yes, Madre?" Miguel said.

"You are angry," she said.

"No, Madre. I could never be angry with you." Miguel said.

"Not with me, my son. You are angry at the world. It seeps out of you like sweat."

"I am past anger, Madre." Miguel said.

"That would be good. God would forgive you. If only what you say were true."

He had never heard her speak like this before. It troubled him. He said, "I would not lie to you, Madre."

"You can and you have. And I have forgiven you. I do not have much time left."

"Madre, do not speak of such things! The doctors—"

She held up her hand to stop him. "The doctors know that I am dying. They are too afraid of you to tell you. It is not their fault. I am old. It is the way of life, Miguel."

"I will find new doctors." Miguel said.

"And they will lie to you as well. No. No more doctors. No more medicine. But that is not what I want to talk with you about."

She coughed, and he helped her sit up until her lungs cleared.

"I want your promise," she said. "You fight for what you believe in. That is good and honorable. But you cannot turn to violence, Miguel. If you do, you are no better than those who oppress us."

"Madre . . ."

"No," she said. "You cannot go down this road. Violence cannot be undone."

Miguel said nothing. The truth of it was, he already

lied to her. He had committed many acts of violence. He was a revolutionary. A bandit. A rebel. A killer. He was La Vibora—the Viper. And he had much more killing to do. Until his people were free. That is what a revolutionary did.

"Sometimes the road is not a peaceful one, Madre," he said.

"This is true," she said. "But you have many gifts, Miguel. Your words and deeds are legendary. To many, you are a hero. Do not become a killer. Promise me."

He took her hand but said nothing.

"Promise me, Miguel," she begged.

"I promise, Madre," he said.

She visibly relaxed. Her breathing became regular, and she slipped into a deep sleep. It was as if delivering this message allowed her to rest.

He stood and left the building. He hated lying to his mother. It was like a punch in the stomach. It was a sin. May God forgive him. But he could not turn back now.

La Vibora was going to start a war. He was going to kill the United States Ambassador to Venezuela.

Miguel said a prayer asking for forgiveness for the lie he had told his mother. And a prayer asking for strength in the fight to come.

◉ CHAPTER 2

The mortar shell explosion sounded too close.

"Cover!" Chief Master Sergeant "Mako" Marks said.

There were three injured marines on the ground.
Mako, Master Sergeant Garcia, and Airman Bashir
were each tending the patients. At the sound of the
explosion, each of the PJs, or Air Force Pararescuemen,
shielded the patients with their own bodies.

As the dirt stopped flying, they returned to their
work. Machine gun fire popped all around them. Tracer
rounds lit up the sky over their heads.

"Blood sweep!" Mako said.

"Clear!" Garcia said.

"Superficial wound on back shoulder!" Bashir said.

Quickly and methodically, the PJs tended to their
patients. The Pave Hawk helicopter waited a short
distance away. Time was the enemy. Getting the
patients to hospitals within sixty minutes from the

time injuries occurred greatly improved their chances for survival.

The PJs ran their gloved hands over the patients. In a hot landing zone, it was easy to miss wounds. Some bullets passed completely through bodies. Shrapnel struck and stuck almost anywhere. The blood sweep was essential and often saved lives.

"Blood pressure dropping!" Garcia said.

"What's wrong?" Mako said. "What's causing it?"

"I don't know," said Garcia. "There are no further wounds that I can see. It could be internal bleeding.

Another mortar round exploded, and the PJs hunched over their patients. They needed to keep wounds as clean as possible, and their patients from being further injured.

"We need to get them out of here," Mako shouted over the noise. "Give him ten ccs of Ovateam. Bashir and I will load the Cat Alphas. We'll see if he's stable by the time we get there."

"Roger that," Garcia said.

Garcia started the injection. Mako and Bashir got their patients on stretchers. They were safely loaded into the chopper. Mako went back to check on Garcia's patient.

"His blood pressure is stable," Garcia said.

"Then let's get him loaded on the helicopter," Mako said.

A voice came over the loudspeaker. It was Lieutenant Jamal Jenkins, the squad's Combat Rescue Officer. "Okay. Shut it down. Shut it down."

The lights turned on. They were inside a converted hangar at Lackland Air Force base in Texas. It had been made to look like an actual desert for a test. The special effects for the gunfire and mortars made it look like a movie set.

Jenkins walked over from the command post. "All right everyone," he said. "That's all for today. Get some rest. We'll be right back here tomorrow at zero eight hundred for more training."

Jenkins walked over to Mako. Chief Master Sergeant Mako was the highest-ranking member of the squad after Jenkins.

"Mako, I'd like to see you in my office tomorrow at zero seven hundred," he said.

"Yes, sir!'" Mako said. He turned to help one of the volunteer marines to his feet. Jenkins left the hangar and headed for his quarters.

The next morning, Mako arrived at Lieutenant Jamal Jenkins' office at 6:50. He considered ten minutes early as being "on time."

"Come in, sergeant," Jenkins said.

Mako came to attention in front of Jenkins' desk. His uniform was neatly pressed, and his boots shone brightly. Even his dark blue PJ beret was placed perfectly on his head. Mako had been a PJ for fifteen years, Jenkins for six. Jenkins thought Mako was the finest PJ he had met. But he had a tendency to go "cowboy" and do his own thing on some missions.

"Mako, during last night's training," Jenkins said, "you ordered Sergeant Garcia to give Ovateam to a patient to stabilize him."

"Yes, sir." Mako said.

"I have made clear I don't want us using this drug," Jenkins said. "Yet you used it. Why?"

"Sir, given the situation, I felt the reward outweighed the risks. We carry Ovateam in our med kits. If we're not going to use it, we shouldn't carry it."

"I get your point, Mako," Jenkins said. "Believe me, I do. But I gave an order. You countermanded it. I can't

have that from my chief master sergeant. This was just a training exercise. What if it were a mission?"

"Sir, if it were a mission, I would make the exact same call. The simulation said that marine had taken a hit from an IED. His body armor saved him. But he was wounded and time was running out. It was an easy call to make."

"But the risk . . ." Jenkins let his words trail off.

"Sir, every soldier and marine in a combat zone is taking risks twenty-four-seven," Mako said. "It's a part of my job. They look to PJs to pull their bacon out of the fire. It was a risk to use Ovateam. But same scenario in live combat? I'd do it again sir."

"So, you would cut the CRO out of the equation?" Jenkins said.

"No, sir, only the bad ones," Mako said.

Despite the seriousness of the situation, Jenkins had to stifle a laugh. "Go on," Jenkins said. "I know you've got more to say. Speak freely."

"Sir, you are the CRO, the Combat Rescue Officer. You are directing the mission from the base and not the field."

"What does that have to do with anything?" Jenkins asked.

"Sir," said Mako, "as Chief Master Sergeant of this unit, I am your eyes and ears on the ground. Is that correct?"

"Yes." Jenkins said.

"You weren't there, sir," Mako said. "Given the symptoms and how much time was left in the Golden Hour, I had to make a call. We had to give the patient Ovateam. His blood pressure was too low. The patient wouldn't have been able to take pain medication without it. Even Sandman agreed."

Sandman was Sergeant Garcia's nickname. He was the PJ team's best medic and carried a lot of respect.

"Were you willing to take the risk if his blood pressure spiked and he had a stroke?" Jenkins asked.

"Sir," Mako said, "taking risks is what we do. I was senior NCO on the ground, I made a call. As I see it, that's my job. Sir."

Jenkins leaned back in his desk chair. Mako was the best PJ he'd ever served with. Mako was technically right. He was on the ground. Jenkins, as the combat rescue officer, was in the operations center. In a real mission, he watched things unfold through body cameras and drone footage. But they didn't always show everything. Orders had to be followed.

What if he had given the wrong order? It was just a simulation. They couldn't have miscommunication like this.

"Mako," Jenkins said, "sit down. At ease. Please."

The sergeant sat in the chair opposite the desk. To Jenkins he looked like he was still at attention.

"Let's figure this out," Jenkins said.

"Yes, sir," Mako said.

"What's your assessment of this situation?" Jenkins asked.

"Truthfully, sir," said Mako, "I think you made a mistake."

"A mistake," said Jenkins. He leaned forward and looked Mako in the eye.

"Yes, sir," said Mako.

For some reason, the words stung Jenkins. He knew he wasn't perfect. Human beings make mistakes. But this was a training exercise, which made the accusation even worse. It's one thing to make a mistake when you're in a dire situation.

Guns going off.

Explosions.

Injured patients on the verge of bleeding out.

Then, you are making life-or-death decisions. In

those cases, with intense pressure, mistakes were more likely to happen. But the whole point of the exercise was to prepare for real-world missions. Screwing up during training was somehow worse.

Jenkins took a deep breath. Maybe Mako had a point.

Mako looked at his commanding officer. He didn't like what he saw.

"Sir?" Mako said.

"Yes?" Jenkins asked.

"No disrespect intended, sir," Mako said, "but you're being way too hard on yourself."

"Is that right?"

"Yes, sir," said Mako. "Sir, you're in the top three CROs I've served with in fifteen years as a PJ. You strive for perfection. That's great. Everyone should. But the fact is, we're not perfect.

"Sir, if this had been a real mission I would have made the same call," Mako said. "If you want to punish me for it, so be it. But like I said. If that happened again, I would do the same thing."

Jenkins gazed off out the window of his office. "You think I'm the one that made a mistake here?" Jenkins said.

"Yes, sir," said Mako. "I do. And I'm okay with it. In fact, I'm glad you called me on it."

"Now you've really lost me, Mako," Jenkins said.

"You called me on it. We're clearing the air. We rely on each other. We won't always agree. If we tear a plan apart to find weak spots, we make our plans stronger. Sir."

Mako was still sitting straight up in the chair.

"Mako," Jenkins said. "I've got to say. You are a wonder."

"Yes, sir," said Mako. "That's obvious, isn't it?"

Now Jenkins laughed out loud.

"All right," said Jenkins. "Consider this matter closed. But in the future, if you think I'm wrong, I'd appreciate if you talk to me first, conditions permitting, before you disobey an order. Is that clear?"

"Crystal, sir." Mako said.

"Dismissed," Jenkins said.

Mako got up and walked to the office door.

"Mako?" Jenkins asked.

"Sir?" Mako turned.

"You said I was the third best CRO you ever served with," said Jenkins. "Who were the first and second best?"

"Can't tell you, sir. It's classified." Mako said.

Mako grinned as he left the office, quietly shutting the door. Jenkins smiled as he looked out the window. A feeling rolled over him then. The sun was bright. It was going to be a hot Texas day. In the past few months, his unit had been in Afghanistan and Alaska. Two completely different places.

He felt like they would be going somewhere else. Soon. Someplace unlike Afghanistan and Alaska. That's what they did.

Jenkins just wished whatever was going to happen would happen. So they could go and fix it. Save lives.

"These things we do," Jenkins said to himself.

Jenkins couldn't have guessed about the nature of the events leading to his next mission that were already underway.

Miguel Ramos, the Viper, fidgeted with nervous energy as he drove the truck. He had not visited the capital city of Caracas, Venezuela, for many weeks. The city had been ready to explode then. The government issued a reward for turning him in. They considered him a terrorist.

The price on his head changed everything. He no longer knew who to trust. Even his most devoted followers could turn on him. In truth, he couldn't blame them. With money, they might be able to buy food. It would ensure another few weeks of life for them and their children. That was how far Venezuela had fallen. It was why people were ready to take to the streets and fight.

The United States viewed the situation in the country as unstable. They decided to recall their ambassador. Their embassy would still remain open.

But they wanted the ambassador and his staff returned to America. The United Nations threatened to send in peacekeeping troops. The Venezuelan president went on radio and television.

"Any attempt to send troops into our country," the Venezuelan president said, "will be met with the full might of our military. We will not allow invaders to determine the destiny of Venezuela."

The Viper was sick of all of the words. Tired of the politicians who robbed his country, who sucked it dry and left nothing behind for his people. No food. No jobs. No future. No hope.

Miguel wanted change. The easiest way for that was war. The Venezuelan military could control the people. But if the United States or one of its allies were provoked into a war, the Viper thought that the Venezuelan military would crumble like a stale cracker.

Then he would be there to offer an alternative. A government that served the people. He would rule the country without the corruption and crime of the current leaders. It would be a great day.

Miguel was parked in the truck, down a side street from the American Embassy. It was the perfect spot to watch for the Ambassador's motorcade. His truck had a cab on the back. It looked like a rental moving truck.

Finally, he saw activity.

The iron gates opened and two large, black SUVs pull through and onto the street. He knew they were headed to the airport. Miguel started following at a discreet distance, keeping them in sight.

The first vehicle most likely carried the ambassador and his family. The next vehicle probably carried a heavily armed squad of Diplomatic Security Service agents. In United States Law Enforcement, DSS agents were some of the most highly trained and lethal. They trained to be ready for anything from an assassination attempt to a full-on terrorist attack.

The Viper was not worried about them at the moment.

City traffic was light. Gasoline prices had risen to the point that people could not afford to drive—not unless it was an absolute emergency. Following at a safe distance, he soon trailed the two SUVs onto the expressway that led to the airport. They drove through the airport to the area for private aircraft. A modified Boeing 707 sat on the tarmac. It awaited passengers.

The Viper kept driving. He turned on a street that ran perpendicular to the runway. Then he turned left, heading away from the airport. He drove for five miles. He didn't want witnesses to see what he was about to do. At last he found the deserted spot. It had overgrown brush and debris. He pulled the truck in and opened the cab.

The back of the truck concealed a surface-to-air missile system. It had not been used in some time. Still, it was functional. He had done the calculations. At this spot, the plane should be high enough to hit. But it wouldn't be high enough that it would have time to deploy countermeasures to stop the missile from reaching its target.

Miguel waited. He grew more nervous by the minute. What if someone wandered by and spotted him? Worse yet, what if someone recognized him? It could ruin everything.

Checking his watch, he saw that it was past the scheduled departure time. That may have been intentional. If the DSS agents had learned of a threat, they would throw the ambassador's schedule off intentionally. They would try to keep any potential assassins from knowing when and where he was.

There. Off in the distance. He heard a plane.

He had time. Carefully he pushed buttons on the

console to turn the guidance system on. He had only one heat-seeking missile. He could not miss.

At last the plane appeared on the horizon. It was climbing steadily at a more severe angle than usual. It worked to the Viper's advantage. He looked at the console. He watched as the altitude on the target slowly changed.

When the plane was at 15,000 feet and a distance of one and a half miles from his location, he pressed a button that fired the missile.

He was surprised and somewhat shocked at the power of the single missile. The truck shook on its suspension. The back blast from the missile was hot and intense. For a moment, it looked like it was hanging suspended in the air. Then it whizzed away, headed straight for the aircraft.

In seconds, it hit the plane, taking out the starboard engine. The plane had no time to release any countermeasures or take evasive action. It was like a wounded duck struck by a hunter.

The plane shuddered. Part of the right wing peeled away. Fire poured out of the engine. What would the pilot do? Would he attempt to return to the airport? Would he try an emergency landing somewhere else?

Miguel had planned carefully. At that altitude, the pilot could only glide over the jungle. He would not have the power or stability to try and return to the airport. The plane would go down somewhere in a large, mostly deserted part of Venezuela.

Miguel sent a text on his cell phone. The message was just one word: Go.

His followers in Caracas were waiting for his signal. Their mission was to attack a group of protesters in the city. They had nothing against these particular protesters today. It was to create a diversion.

The government would need to end the riot. Their resources would be stretched thin. The riot would leave them with fewer assets to assign to searching for the downed plane.

In the jungle, he had several groups stationed along the flight path of the ambassador's plane. If it crashed there and there were survivors, the Viper's men would seize them and be gone quickly. They would vanish before any government or military forces could reach the crash site.

The Viper started the truck and pulled out of the brushy area. Soon he was back on the freeway. As he drove, he waited for word from his comrades.

As the miles passed, he grew more anxious. He called a few of his team leaders. No word on the plane. Had the pilot managed to somehow return to the airport? He turned on the truck's radio to a local news station. The reports cut back and forth between the news of the riots in the streets and the plane hit by a missile. After listening a while, he determined that the plane did not return to the airport.

"La Vibora! La Vibora!" a voice he recognized as Andres' came over the handheld radio.

"Do not call me that name when you are transmitting!" said the Viper. "What is it?"

"Apologies, señor," said Andres. "We have found the plane. It is an hour away from Caracas."

"What are the coordinates?" asked the Viper.

Andres replied. Miguel wrote them onto a small piece of paper.

"Excellent, Andres," said the Viper. "Take your men and head to the crash site immediately. Don't do anything until I get there."

"Si!" Andres replied. "But what if the military appears?"

"Use your judgment," The Viper said, "If they arrive in force and there are too many opposing you, take them to the camp as we discussed. If it is a small force . . . kill them."

There was no reply.

"Andres?" The Viper asked.

"Yes, señor?" Andres asked.

"Do you understand my instructions?"

"Yes, La Vib—Miguel. I understand."

"Good," said the Viper. "Do not disappoint me."

Miguel pressed on the gas. The truck sped down the freeway. There was much to do.

◎ CHAPTER 4

Location: Lackland Air Force Base
            San Antonio, Texas
Date: June 8th
Time: 0400 hours

"Let's go, let's go!" Mako walked down the hallway of the barracks banging on doors and rattling trash cans. He made noise with anything he could get his hands on. Chief Master Sergeant Phil "Mako" Marks did not believe in slowly easing into the day. He preferred the direct, abrupt approach.

As usual, Senior Airman Ahmad Bashir was the first to poke his head out of his sleeping area.

"What's up, sarge?" Bashir asked.

"Briefing room, ten minutes," Mako barked. "Which means be there in five minutes!"

"Is it a mission?" Bashir asked. Somehow, he was already wearing his uniform.

Mako wondered if he didn't sleep in it. "I don't know, Bash," Mako said. "All I was told was to get you bunch of lazy bums to the briefing room in ten minutes. Something tells me Loot ain't gonna be handing out candy."

Sergeant Garcia staggered out of his cubby. "Why us? If there's a mission somewhere, let the SEALS handle it. We shouldn't have to go on a mission before 10:00 a.m."

"Sergeant Garcia," Mako said, "did you just imply that our US Navy brethren special operators, also known as SEALS, should handle a mission instead of the PJs? The finest, bravest, sharpest point on the spear of American democracy? Please tell me you didn't say that, sergeant. It would pain me to see you taking extra PT and peeling potatoes for the next three months."

Garcia raised his hands. He yawned. "Ease up, sergeant. All I'm suggesting is maybe we could just divide up the workday. Let our NAVY brothers take the morning shift. That's all I'm saying." Garcia was grinning.

"Haul your can to the briefing room right now," Mako said.

"Yes, Sergeant," Garcia said.

Being a sergeant, Garcia was nearly the same rank as Mako. Garcia could joke with him a little bit. But only a little. Mako took his job very seriously. He got away with the joking because Mako knew that Garcia was good at his job as well.

All the other PJs in the squad were stirring now. It was hard to sleep when you had a raving lunatic loose in your barracks. They dressed and were seated in the briefing room well before Mako's five-minute time limit had passed.

When they arrived there, they found Lieutenant Jenkins waiting. There were several photos and maps projected on a smart screen. Jenkins was studying a briefing book. There was a pot of coffee on the table. They all helped themselves to a cup.

"Gentlemen," Jenkins said. "We are being deployed near the equator. We will be in the air in one hour. We take rucks and equipment for a jungle climate. This mission will also require we parachute in. If we are able to recover our people, we will attempt extraction by chopper. If not, we walk them out. That could include carrying casualties."

"What is the mission, sir?" Sergeant Frank George asked.

Jenkins pointed to the screen.

"Two hours ago," Jenkins said, "a United States

Department of State aircraft was shot down by a surface-to-air missile. It was taking off from the airport in Venezuela. On board were the Ambassador and his wife, a few staffers, and three members of the Department of State Security Service,"

"How does this involve us?" Garcia asked. "Why not marines or rangers?"

"I assume, Sergeant," Mako said, "it involves us because those are our orders." He still did not appreciate Garcia's joke about the SEALS earlier.

Jenkins looked at the two men for a moment.

"Something going on here?" Jenkins asked.

"No, sir," Garcia said. "Just curious."

"With the potential for casualties and injuries, they want us going in," Jenkins said. "But I'm also going to tell you that things may get hot. A Venezuelan rebel group called the Army of Venom is claiming responsibility for the attack."

"Excuse me, sir," Airman Bashir said. "But won't Venezuelan authorities be on site before we can reach them?"

"Good question, airman," Jenkins said. "Ordinarily, yes. But things in Venezuela are . . . currently unstable. There are riots in the streets on a daily basis. Their economy is in shreds. At the time the plane was hit, a massive riot broke out in the streets of Caracas, the capital city."

"Any intel on the plane's suspected location?" Mako asked.

"That's another problem," Jenkins said. "With its fight path, it was headed from the airport toward the east. Speculation is the missile damaged an engine and the frame. We suspect it had to put down in the jungle somewhere. There's been unusual cloud cover over the region for the past few days. We've got nothing by satellite. The transponder on the plane wasn't working, or may have been sabotaged."

"So, we have no idea where they are?" Airman Phil Gage said.

"A rough idea. A couple hundred square miles of jungle," Jenkins said.

"Have we tried reconnaissance planes?" George asked.

"Negative," Jenkins said. "We were getting the Ambassador out of there. Relations between the United States and Venezuela were getting worse quickly. Sending in recon planes could ruin them. That's why we're going in. At night, on the down low."

Jenkins looked around the table. Each member of the squad was intently studying the briefing books. Getting themselves prepared. Combing over the intelligence reports. Any little piece of information could make the difference during a mission. They were all business.

"One more thing," Jenkins said. "Intel sources have an included a profile on the Army of Venom. It's run by some patriot named Ramos. They might have gotten to the plane and grabbed any survivors. They know the jungle, and they're well armed. So there is the potential for shooting here. Take extra ammo and make sure your weapons are doubly clean. Humidity in the jungle can harm them, just like sand in the desert."

Jenkins looked at his watch. "OK, wheels up in forty-five. Let's go."

The PJs started toward the door.

"One more thing. Gage? Make sure you bring your sniper rifle. I have a feeling it might come in handy," Jenkins said.

"I never leave home without it, sir," Gage said. He saluted and left the room.

Miguel Ramos cursed his luck.

The ambassador's plane had an exceptional pilot. They may not have been able to turn the plane back to the airport. In fact, the aircraft was damaged in a way that it could only fly in a straight line and glide, as several systems lost power. It was hard to control.

The aircrew did a masterful job holding the plane together. They were still going to make a hard landing.

They ended up going down in the Guiana Highlands in one of Venezuela's national parks. It was an area that was marked by strange geologic formations called tepuis. Tepuis were mountains that were flat on the top. The reason these strange mountains were flat was a mystery. They were large and tall. Some of them towered so high that clouds obscured their peaks. The ambassador's plane had landed on top of one of the tepuis.

Miguel Ramos had not planned for this. The only advantage it had is that it would take any government forces longer to get there. Miguel and his rebel force were closer. But they would spend extra time getting to the crash site. And if there were injured to evacuate and hold for ransom, it would be difficult to move them down from the tepuis.

Time was Miguel's enemy now.

The United States government would immediately demand answers. They would insist on sending in retrieval teams. The Venezuelan government would deny them. They would not miss a propaganda opportunity, showing them coming to the rescue of any American survivors. It would be a public relations victory they would not allow to pass.

Miguel drove the truck to a side street in Caracas next to a factory. It was important the truck not be found. Giving up the surface-to-air missile control system was a difficult blow. But it was hard to find the missiles, and they were expensive. The launcher was useless without missiles. He had accomplished his goal with that truck. If he needed another missile launcher, he would find a way to get one. La Vibora always found a way.

The factory where he parked the truck was deserted. It had been closed for years and was fairly well isolated. From the back of the truck, he carefully removed a crate from the rear compartment. It was full of C4 plastic explosives. It took him nearly thirty minutes to pack the C4 around throughout the truck. He attached the detonator and set the timer to three minutes.

Miguel jogged away to a safe distance and watched. Exactly three minutes later ,the explosion thundered. The noise was deafening. When he heard chunks of metal hitting the ground, he was sure the truck and its cargo were destroyed.

Miguel continued on toward a bus stop. He would take a bus to where he left his jeep. Once on the bus, he thought again about the official response to the accident. The government was unreliable. Yet they could not take advantage of this opportunity he had created for the movement.

Miguel had many followers and fairly extensive resources. But not as many as he made the government believe. There was not much money in being a revolutionary. Weapons and equipment were hard to come by, even when you had the money. But he was smart. He knew the jungle. And he and his forces were far nimbler than the government.

Miguel exited the bus at a downtown parking garage. Several streets away, he could hear the sounds of sirens and large crowds of people shouting. His plan to start the riot had worked wonderfully. He found his car.

Driving up the mountains to the compound took another hour. Once he reached it, he gathered up his equipment. Plenty of ammunition, food, and water. He had several rocket-propelled-grenade launchers. There were a number of automatic weapons and grenades in the armory.

Transportation to the crash site was the problem. They would not be able to drive there in time. His closest team was more than 200 kilometers away.

His phone beeped.

"Yes, Andres?" Miguel said.

"Our team reports smoke coming from the crash site," Andres said. "They are moving fast, and are within one hundred and thirty kilometers of the plane's location."

"That is excellent news," Miguel said. "You must make it clear to them they must get there fast."

"Yes, señor," Andres said. "The problem will be climbing the mountain. The terrain is rugged. It will slow us down."

"I am on my way to you now," Miguel said. "Tell the men to have faith. These next days will bring us a great victory."

Miguel disconnected the call. He stood there for a moment. There were two things he needed to do.

The first was that he needed to say goodbye to his mother.

The second: He had to steal a helicopter.

With a pilot.

◎ CHAPTER 6

Location: Near Venezuela
Date: June 8th
Time: 1800 hours

Airmen Gage and Bashir sat in the back of the
C-130, talking as they waited to reach the drop zone.

"Bash, do you ever think what we do is crazy?"
Gage asked.

"What do you mean?" Bashir said.

"I mean think about it," Gage said. "We were just
in Alaska. In the middle of one of the worst blizzards
in the history of blizzards. Falling down mountains,
nearly freezing to death, and dodging polar bears."

"I don't think there were any polar bears," Bashir
said. "If there were, we probably wouldn't be here now."

"That's not what I mean," Gage said. "Look at us
now. Who jumps out of a perfectly good airplane? If
the engines were on fire, that'd be one thing. But it's
humming like a top. And we're going to jump out of it.
Into a hot, stinky jungle. And in the darkness, no less."

Gage shook his head.

Bashir smiled. He knew parachuting was Gage's least favorite part of being a PJ. Not that he thought Gage was scared. Bashir knew that Gage was fearless. But PJs were human beings. And all human beings had likes and dislikes.

"Well, look at it this way, Gage," Bashir said. "Maybe you'll get to bring some bad guys to justice this time."

Gage rolled his eyes.

For men who were used to action, long plane rides were the worst. It was a constant war against boredom. In Afghanistan, every mission involved riding in on a chopper to extract wounded. Everyone was on edge and scanning the ground for enemy fire.

Almost every landing zone in Afghanistan held some kind of danger. The Taliban was notorious for waiting for any type of medical evacuation aircraft to arrive. Then they would launch a furious assault trying to kill as many of the rescue personnel as they could. There were few, if any, parachute drops.

On a long plane ride like this one, a PJ could lose focus. Bashir looked around. Lieutenant Jenkins was reviewing the briefing book for the fifteenth time. Sergeants Garcia and George were playing cards.

Mako was sound asleep, his mouth wide open. Every so often he would twist in his seat and mumble something. Mako was a big believer in getting sleep whenever possible. PJs sometimes had to be awake for three days straight.

Bashir would've liked a snooze. But jumps made Gage nervous, so he talked to Bashir—a lot. Gage was Bashir's best friend in the unit. But every once in a while, he wished his friend would let him catch a little sleep.

The pilot's voice came over the intercom: "Drop zone in thirty. Repeat. Drop zone in thirty."

The space inside the C-130 became a buzzing beehive of activity. Mako was instantly awake and on his feet. Everyone went straight to their jobs. Putting on rucks, stepping into parachute harnesses, and gathering equipment. Each PJ double-checked his own gear first, then took turns examining each other's. All the pieces and parts were hooked up and attached correctly.

"Fifteen minutes to drop zone," the pilot said.

Everyone attached rigs to the static line running the length of the C-130. This was a low-altitude drop. The static line would automatically deploy their chutes once they were safely out of the aircraft.

The last few minutes of waiting always seemed like hours. Every man watched for the green light to go on. That was the signal to jump.

"Five minutes," the pilot's voice came over the speakers.

"Everyone, heads up," Jenkins said. "Make sure you have the coordinates to the rally point in your GPSes. We're jumping into a jungle at night. Jungles mean trees. Not to mention any wild animals that are out there. Use your night-vision system to look for clearings. Why do we do this?"

"So that others may live!" the squad answered back.

"Hooah!" they all shouted.

The green light buzzed on. The jumpmaster shouted, "Go, go, go!"

Jenkins was the first out of the plane. One by one the PJs followed him, floating gently into the night sky.

CHAPTER 7

Location: The Guinea Highlands, Venezuela
Date: June 8th
Time: 2000 hours

The helicopter landed with a jolt. Miguel had to admit the pilot did a masterful job landing in such difficult terrain. Then again, his concentration was complete. Because Miguel had a gun pointed at him.

"Shut down the engines," Miguel said. The pilot did as he was ordered, and the engine whined to a stop. From the treeline, he saw his men emerge, moving toward the chopper. Up ahead he could see the tepui where the plane crashed. The top of the mountain was hidden under heavy clouds. This particular tepui was over 7,000 feet tall.

Jose, one of his most trusted men, was leading this particular group of Miguel's army.

He grasped Miguel's hand firmly. "Hola, señor," he said.

"Hello, Jose. It has been too long. You look well," Miguel said.

"We are ready to scale the summit," Jose said. "One of the men claims to know a trail that leads to the top. It will be a difficult climb, but we should arrive there in a few hours."

"Excellent. And you are sure this is where the plane landed?" Miguel asked.

"Si, señor. The plane is there," Jose said.

Miguel stopped to consider his options for a moment. The easy thing to do would be to take the helicopter to the top and take as many hostages as they could carry. However, if there were survivors, some of them could be Marines or Department of State Security agents. They would be heavily armed. He had gone up against both groups before. They were dangerous opponents. Risking a firefight there would be foolish.

Unless he came up with a way to outsmart them.

The other option was to send men to the top. Let them find out what conditions were. Once they had secured any hostages, the helicopter could fly up and take them away. He had to consider fuel. And the possibility that if the security detail survived, they might disable the helicopter with gunfire.

This was one of the most remote areas in the

world. Any survivors of the crash would not be able to call for help. There would be no cellphone coverage. Their satellite phones would do them no good. They were still inside Venezuela. The government would not allow any other rescuers to help them. And the government authorities would not be able to mount a rescue for hours.

If only the plane had not crashed on top of the tepui. Miguel was an educated man. But the superstitious side of him saw this as a bad omen. This part of Venezuela was called the Guinea Highlands. Tepuis dotted the countryside here. Some of the tallest ones had large sinkholes on the top. Others were so high they had their own weather and ecosystems at the peak. The native tribes who once lived here considered them sacred.

Miguel Ramos was La Vibora—The Viper. He was strong and smart. Still he was Venezuelan enough to feel the mystical pull of this place. Shaking his head, he tried to focus.

In the end, he decided to leave three of Jose's men to guard the chopper. Miguel and his men would scale the mountain. They would come upon the wreck silently. Any survivors could be captured by surprise.

Even if there were no survivors, Miguel and his men could retrieve the ambassador's body and hold it for ransom. It would still be a victory for the Army of Venom.

"Jose, I want you to stay behind and guard the chopper," Manuel said. "Keep it hidden in case anyone flies over. Keep two men. The others will go with me. Once there, when we have secured the crash site, I will signal you on the radio. Bring the helicopter to the summit. We will take the hostages first. Any who are too injured we will leave behind. When the government gets around to mounting a rescue party, they can take care of them."

"What if someone shows up? A rescue party or government troops?" Jose asked.

"If that happens, kill the pilot and leave as quickly as possible. If they follow, lose them in the jungle," Miguel said. "Unless something happens, maintain radio silence. Do not contact me for any reason except the most extreme emergency. I will need to keep the radio on, but we may need to be silent in our approach. Understood?"

"Si, mi amigo," Jose replied. "Yes, my friend."

Miguel looked at the four men who would

accompany him to the summit. The man who knew the way was Hermano. He took point as they made their way toward the tepui. It was going to be a dangerous trip.

But La Vibora smiled.

It would be worth it.

◉ CHAPTER 8

The jump went wrong right away. Low altitude was always riskier. As Mako liked to say, "On a low jump, the ground is closer." Right after they cleared the airplane, a wind gust came out of nowhere. The forecast called for light winds. With their chutes already deployed, the squad was being blown farther away from the intended LZ.

Sergeant George's lines got tangled, and he started falling at a faster rate. The other PJs were helpless. He was going to land hard.

"George! George!" Mako shouted over the radio. "Cut your lines! Use the reserve chute! Do it now!"

Sergeant George didn't respond.

"George! Reply, over!" Mako said.

"Easy, Mako," Lieutenant Jenkins said.

"Sergeant George, if you hear me, answer," Jenkins said over the comm.

There was no response. Either George's ear piece was out, or he was too busy trying to save his own life. They could see him in the moonlight. He was approximately one thousand feet below them.

"Lieutenant, I'm going to cut my chute and dive to him," Mako said. "We'll double up on my reserve and make it down that way."

"Negative, Mako. I say again. Negative. That is a direct order," Lieutenant Jenkins said.

The comm exploded with Mako's curses.

"Take it easy, chief master sergeant. Sergeant George is an experienced PJ," Jenkins said. "He knows what to do."

The seconds ticked by, and they watched. George was plummeting to the earth.

"He's going to be messed up bad when he hits the ground," Airman Gage said to no one in particular.

Each PJ was watching and feeling helpless. They gritted their teeth, trying to fight the wind while keeping an eye on their teammate. At the speed he was falling he could still land, and survive. But he would likely suffer serious injuries.

About fifteen hundred feet from the ground, Sergeant George's chute fluttered up into the air. It was immediately whipped away by a rushing wind gust. He had cut the lines. Almost immediately, his reserve chute opened and his descent slowed. It was still too close to the ground, but now he had a better chance.

"George! Sergeant George! Come in!" Mako shouted over the comm.

Still no response. Now the squad had a second problem. Losing communication with George put them in a bind. If he was injured landing, he would be much harder to find with a broken comm unit. They wouldn't be able to trace the signal back to his location.

It felt like the descent was taking an eternity. Sergeant George was just a few hundred feet away from the ground. At least the lines on his reserve chute had not tangled.

The winds were blowing the squad east. Below them they could see George's parachute outlined against the dark jungle. He was desperately trying to steer to a better landing spot. The wind was not helping, and the reserve chutes were not as easy to steer as the main chute.

The squad could only watch him as he crashed through the trees.

"Everybody, look at the landmarks and try to

memorize the terrain where he went down," Mako shouted through the comm. "We're going to have to go to him. Everybody! Eyes on me. We going to try to catch that brushy area thirty degrees to the left of my position. Better to land in brush than hit a tree. Follow me in!"

Each PJ pulled at the handles attached to his parachute. They turned back into the wind, trying to keep it from pushing them farther east. The ground rushed up at them. Their landing area was roughly the size of a football field. It was full of leafy bushes and tall grasses. Thankfully, there were no big trees to worry about. All of them hit the spot except for Garcia. He drifted farther east into the jungle and disappeared in the trees.

"Everybody hide your chutes and huddle up!" Jenkins said.

Once all of them were clear of their parachutes they gathered around the Lieutenant.

"Everyone all right? Anyone injured?" Jenkins asked.

All of the PJs present landed without incident.

"We're going to split up and look for Garcia and . . ." Jenkins said.

"Here he comes now," Gage said.

Sure enough, Garcia emerged from the trees. Spotting them, he jogged over and joined the group.

"You okay, Garcia?" Jenkins asked.

"I'm fine. It just got breezy up there. Would have landed right here, but a little puff of wind blew me off target," Garcia said.

"All right then," Jenkins said. He took a compass reading. "We need to find Sergeant George right away. Double-time. Bashir, take point. Mako, you've got our back. Remember that for all intents and purposes, we are in an enemy combat zone. There are more rebel groups than the Army of Venom in the country. None of them are big fans of the USA. We're going to try and be as quiet as we can, but move fast. Sergeant George may need us. Any questions?"

Jenkins expected none and there weren't. His men were well trained and knew their jobs.

Silently, they turned toward the west. They would head back to the spot Sergeant George landed. He was probably hanging in a tree somewhere, waiting for someone to come and cut him down.

Any type of travel through a jungle was difficult. But on foot it was downright hazardous. Trees with long roots and grasses with leaves sharp enough to cut skin were everywhere. Not to mention, they also needed to keep an eye out for dangerous critters. All of them were ready to bite, sting, squeeze, or poison anyone they got hold of.

Quickly, they hiked their way toward George. It didn't take them long to reach the spot they thought he'd gone down.

"George," Mako said. "You here?"

"Mako, quiet," Jenkins said.

"I was whispering," Mako said.

"Into a megaphone maybe," Jenkins said.

They scanned around with their night-vision goggles. They didn't see him. Jenkins was worrying now. He might be seriously injured. Maybe they had come to the wrong place. One of his men might need serious medical attention.

They moved farther east. Still there was no sign of Sergeant George. Jenkins was now officially worried.

"Loot, over here," Mako hissed.

Jenkins walked to Mako, who was pointing up. Tangled in the trees was a parachute harness. The harnesses were equipped with quick release buckles. If you were stuck in a treetop, you only need to pull on a loop and the harness released.

Sergeant George's empty harness was swaying gently in the breeze.

But Sergeant George was nowhere to be seen.

Miguel's radio crackled. It sounded like a gunshot in the quiet jungle. Feeling his temper flaring, he yanked the radio from his belt.

"Jorge!" he whispered angrily. "I told you, I would contact you when it is time. Why do you break radio silence?"

"So sorry, señor," Jorge said. "But I have news I felt you must know. We came across someone in the jungle. Most unexpectedly. In fact, he was stuck up in a tree."

Miguel sighed deeply, trying to control his temper. Some days he felt he was surrounded by idiots. Jorge was usually a fine soldier. What in the world could have happened to cause him to behave so foolishly?

"*Por el amor de Dios*," he muttered." For the love of God.

"Who, Jorge?" Miguel asked. "Who did you find in

the jungle, so important you decided to defy my orders and break radio silence?"

"We found an *Americano*, señor," Jorge said. He was barely able to contain the excitement in his voice.

Miguel had to admit this was unusual and potentially important news.

"Americano? What is an Americano doing in the jungle here?" Miguel asked.

"*El es un soldado*," Jorge said. "He's a soldier."

Miguel was nearly floored by the news. An American soldier. Here already? How had they gotten clearance from the Venezuelan government for such an operation? He could not imagine the current regime calling for them. Which meant this was most likely some type of special forces operations. Perhaps the Navy SEALS or DELTA force.

"What is his name? What branch of the military does he belong to?" Miguel asked.

"He will not speak. He is very stubborn man. His uniform says United States Air Force," Jorge reported.

Miguel was puzzled. What would the USAF be doing here? Were they actively searching for the ambassador's plane? If there was one American, there likely were more.

"Is he alone?" Miguel asked.

"Currently, yes," Jorge said. "But he keeps looking around as if he is expecting reinforcements. I assume he is part of a larger group."

Miguel was quiet, his brain sorting through all the different possibilities. Jorge was right. This single airman was quite likely part of a larger force. That spelled trouble. And if they were parachuting into the jungle, they could already be at the crash site. Or close to it.

"Where was he found?" Miguel asked.

Jorge provided him with the coordinates. Examining his map, Miguel discovered that those coordinates were along the expected flight path of the plane. Would they abandon their lost airman and continue to the downed plane? Or would they try to find the missing man first? He supposed it depended on how many were sent on this mission. But the American could be a pilot who had to eject for some unknown reason.

"Jorge, is he a pilot?" Miguel asked.

"I don't think so, Vibora," Jorge said. "He was carrying an automatic weapon and a large backpack."

Interesting, Miguel thought.

If he was USAF, but not a downed pilot, he was an Air Force Pararescueman. He had heard about the so-called PJs. He had studied their missions and tactics. A downed plane in an unknown location would be an ideal mission for the PJs. That meant there were undoubtedly more of them already on the ground. What would they do?

Miguel tried to think how he would handle such a situation. He would not leave one of his men behind. His soldiers wouldn't follow him if they believed they would be left behind if things went bad. But they most likely would not abandon the mission either. Miguel guessed that all the Americans on the ground would be divided. One to look for their missing man, the second to find the crash site.

Yes. It made sense. And he would do the same thing. He would lead two of his men to the crash site. The other three would move toward the coordinates where the American was captured. If they found Jorge with their teammate, they would come at him hard. If he sent men that way, he might catch the PJs in a cross fire. The perfect plan.

"Victor," Miguel said to the soldier in his group he trusted the most. "Take Vincente and Ramon and go to these coordinates. Look for more American soldiers. They will be searching for their lost man. I will continue with Hermano and Juan to the summit."

"Si, señor." Victor was tall and lean. An excellent fighter and followed orders to the letter. "What shall we do if we run into any Americans?" he asked.

"Take them alive if possible," Miguel said. "Try to surprise them so they have little choice but to surrender. If not . . . eliminate them." He clicked the microphone on the radio.

"Jorge, Victor, and two men are heading back your way to look for more Americans," Miguel said. "Search the captive. Make sure he does not carry or conceal any tracking devices. If he does, destroy them. If he has a radio, destroy it was well. Keep him alive at all costs. I will take two men and continue to the crash site."

Miguel paused, trying to think of every possibility. He had come too far to let himself be defeated now.

"Jorge, it is quite possible there are more Americans about," Miguel said. "They could be tracking their way to you right now. Be prepared for a firefight. I doubt they will give up their friend so easily. Vincente is on his way to you now. Perhaps you can catch them in a cross fire. But hear me, amigo. You must keep your prisoner alive at all costs. In the end, he may be all we have to use to put our plan in motion."

"Si, señor," Jorge said. "Understood."

Miguel slipped the radio back into the holder on his belt. His men stood tense and ready.

"*Vamanos*," Miguel said. "Let's go."

They melted away into the jungle.

◎ CHAPTER 10

Location: Guinea Highlands, Venezuela
Date: June 8th
Time: 2230 hours

Lieutenant Jenkins and Mako stared at the empty harness. Mako felt his anxiety rising. He worried George might be wandering around hurt. Or that someone—probably a rebel group—had found him. They may have taken him hostage.

"What do you think, Mako? Did he walk off on his own? Or did he have help?" Lieutenant Jenkins asked.

The other members of the squad took up defensive positions around the area. They kept an eye on the jungle in each direction. Mako and Lieutenant Jenkins studied the ground.

Mako stopped to consider the options. George was well trained and understood his job. He was probably headed for the rally point. But he might have run into some rebels. News of the plane crash had likely spread. Any number of groups could be headed toward it.

Mako examined the ground around him. The grass was heavily trampled. Too heavily trampled for one man. He walked the area, studying the ground. He paused when he came upon an area of bent and broken plants and grass. It showed that more than one person had moved through the area.

"Look here, Loot," Mako said.

Jenkins kneeled beside Mako.

"A group came through here. At least two, maybe three. See this?" Mako shined his flashlight on the ground. "That heel print is from a PJ boot. I think someone has got him."

Jenkins studied the ground around the boot print. He decided Mako was right. Someone captured Sergeant George. They could be friendly, but the odds were against it.

Jenkins took a moment to think. The ambassador was his clear priority. But Lieutenant Jamal Jenkins could not leave a man behind. Or in the hands of a potential enemy.

"Okay, Mako, you take Bashir and follow this trail," Jenkins said. "Search first before you attempt any recovery. For all we know, some friendly villagers came along to help him down."

Mako racked the slide on his M-4 rifle.

"I highly doubt it. But I understand your orders, sir," Mako said.

"Great," Jenkins said. "Gage, Garcia, and I will find the plane. After you get him back, if George is able, let us know. Then you can come to our position. Let's maintain radio silence until we find George or the plane. You never can tell who might be listening."

"Roger that," Mako said. He took off through the jungle at a quick pace. Bashir followed behind him as best he could. The others watched them disappear into the darkened jungle.

"Loot?" Sergeant Garcia asked.

"Yes?" Jenkins said.

"You know he's going to do whatever it takes to get George back? Even if it means taking on fifty rebels single handed?" Garcia said.

"Oh, I know," Jenkins said.

"And you're not worried?" Garcia asked.

"No. Not really. I calculate fifty rebels up against Mako is close to a fair fight. If there's more, Bashir ought to be able to handle the rest," Jenkins said.

Garcia paused a minute. "Yeah. You're probably right," he said.

"Let's move," Jenkins said. "Gage, you take point. I'll take the rear."

The three of them retraced their steps, moving back into the jungle to the east. They followed the projected flight path of the plane. Even then, it was easy to get lost in the many square miles of jungle. They might take a route right past the wreckage and never see it.

Moving through a thick, overgrown jungle quietly was not easy. But the three PJs did the best they could. They would lose some stealth for speed. The longer they were on the ground, the better chance they had of being discovered. And it would be hard to tell whether it would be worse for the rebels or the government to learn of their presence.

They were making decent time at least. Jenkins wondered what Mako was up to. There were no explosions or sounds of gunfire so far. That was a good thing. The chances of excitement happening went up about fifty percent with Mako running around on his own. Still, if Jenkins were in Sergeant George's place, he'd want Mako coming after him. Jenkins knew Mako wouldn't quit until he found a way to rescue his lost teammate.

The sky was growing lighter to the east. They turned off their night-vision goggles. That increased their speed moving through the jungle.

Gage was moving at a good pace. Then his right hand went up in a fist. It was the hand single to stop. Jenkins and Garcia halted immediately, each dropping to one knee. They waited with their weapons at the ready.

Gage was standing still about thirty yards away from Garcia. He was turning and twisting his head. As if he were trying to hear something. A few moments later, he crouched and turned back, jogging toward Garcia. Jenkins joined them, and they all ducked beneath the grass.

"Loot," Gage said, "I think there's somebody up ahead of us."

"Are you sure?" Jenkins asked.

"I'm seventy percent sure," Gage said. "I heard movement through the jungle, it didn't sound like an animal. I'm positive I heard voices. As far as I know, there's no wild animals in the Amazon that can talk."

Jenkins peeked up over the grass and strained to listen. At first, he heard nothing. Then he thought there might have been a shout far off in the distance.

"All right," Jenkins said. "Sounds like we've got company. Be extra cautious from here on out. Chances are they're headed the same place we are."

Jenkins stood. He cocked his head and listened again. There it was. The sound of human voices.

He headed straight toward them.

◎ CHAPTER 11

Location: Guinea Highlands, Venezuela
Date: June 9th
Time: 0100 hours

Mako and Bashir kneeled in the underbrush. In a clearing before them, Sergeant George stood with his hands bound behind his back. Three men stood nearby with automatic rifles. There was also a helicopter. A man sat in the pilot's seat. From the distance, they couldn't tell if he was armed or not. But he had the look of someone frightened. Like he wanted to be anywhere else than where he was.

"The pilot doesn't appear highly pleased to be here," Mako said quietly, staring through his binoculars. They only had a few hours of darkness left. They would need to figure out a rescue plan soon.

"But just 'cause he's acting squirrely doesn't mean he's a friendly," Mako said. "He could be a rebel. Maybe this is just his first mission. His body language tells me he's scared of the other guys. But let's keep an eye on him."

"Roger that," Bashir said.

Mako put the glasses to his eyes again, carefully studying each man. "They've all got AKs," Mako said. "Two have sidearms. One has a big machete stuck in his belt. I don't see grenades or any other type of weapon. But they could have some hidden in the bushes up there, for all we know. Sergeant George doesn't appear to be injured. George doesn't have his weapon."

Bashir was getting anxious, waiting for Mako to take action.

"Excuse me, sergeant, but what exactly is our plan here?" Bashir asked.

"To get the sergeant back safe and sound, Bash," Mako replied as he continued studying the rebels and the helicopter.

"Yes, sarge, I understand that," Bashir said. But do we have, you know, like an actual plan, that has steps and goals, ultimately leading to the freedom of Sergeant George?"

"You ask too many questions, Airman Bashir," Mako said.

"You don't have a plan, do you, sarge?" Bashir said.

"I'm currently thinking of our options," Mako said.

"And would you care to share?" Bashir asked.

"I plan on us walking up there and asking them real nice if they would be willing to return our fellow PJ to us," Mako said.

Bashir said nothing. In a way, he thought Mako might actually do that. He busied himself checking his gear and clearing the action on his rifle. If they didn't need to be silent, he would have whistled.

"All right. Here's what we're going to do," Mako said after a moment. "You go left and come up on their flank. I'm going straight in and use my diplomatic skills to convince them to surrender Sergeant George."

"Uh, sarge," Bashir said. "No offense, but you don't have any diplomatic skills."

"That's the whole point. You got fifteen minutes, starting now." Mako pressed the timer function on his watch. "Get into position, and if they start shooting, shoot back. Try not to hit the sergeant. Or me."

"Yes, chief master sergeant. Understood," Bashir said. He hurried away into the underbrush.

Mako checked his M-4 rifle. He removed and examined the clip and snapped it back into place. He disengaged the safety. He kept track of the time on his watch. It seemed to take forever, but the fifteen minutes finally passed. Mako crept cautiously forward until he was at the exact edge of the clearing. He didn't speak Spanish, but he could hear the three armed men talking in low tones to each other. With several deep breaths, he launched himself forward.

"Hands up!" Mako said. The three men could not have been more startled, if a ghost had risen up from the ground and tapped them on the shoulder. They jumped and fumbled at their guns.

"*Manos arriba! Manos arriba!*" Mako said. "Hands up!"

Mako had learned a few Spanish phrases from Sergeant Garcia. Some simple commands and orders. It was useful in situations like this. Still caught off guard, the men didn't know how to react.

During his time in the PJs, Mako learned that when things went bad, time seemed to slow down. He never understood why. Maybe it had to do with the rush of adrenaline, the chemical that gave your mind and body an extra boost of strength and awareness. For Mako, each movement and event occurred in slow motion. Everything around him became clearer and sharply focused.

The men ignored his instructions to raise their hands. Each of them were grabbing at their guns.

"Don't do it!" Mako shouted.

It was too late. The man standing closest to Mako raised his weapon. Mako fired and the man went down. The other two men were already down. Sergeant George lay on top of one of them, struggling to keep the man under control. Which was difficult with his hands bound behind his back.

The other man had been shot. Bashir emerged from the brush into the clearing, giving Mako the thumbs-up. The helicopter pilot had his hands up and was screaming in Spanish. Given Mako's limited knowledge of the language, it appeared he was more than willing to surrender.

Mako checked the two men. They were both both dead. Bashir freed Sergeant George, then covered the pilot who still had his hands up and the third man George had taken out. Mako handed George's captured M-4 back to him.

"Took you long enough," George said.

"Obviously you need to brush up on your parachuting skills," Mako said. Bashir secured the third man with zip ties on his hands. The man looked angry. The pilot sat in the seat with his hands over his head. His eyes were closed and he was praying rapidly.

Mako approached him slowly, hoping not to scare him any more. The man prayed harder.

"*Habla inglés?*" Mako asked him. "Do you speak English?"

The man stopped praying. With one hand still over his head, he held the fingers on his other hand about an inch apart.

"A little? You speak a little English?" Mako asked.

The man nodded repeatedly. "Si, señor, si. Small English."

"Get down," Mako waved the barrel of his rifle at the man. He scurried down from the chopper.

"Can you fly this bird?" Mako asked him.

The man looked back confused.

"What's your name?" Mako pointed to himself. "Mako," he said.

"Si, Mako," the man pronounced it with a heavy accent. "*Me llamo es Paulo.*"

"Can you fly this . . ." Mako was interrupted by Airman Bashir who began communicating with the man in fluent Spanish. At least it sounded fluent to Mako. He stared at Bashir, eyes clinching in surprise.

"When did you learn Spanish, Bash?" Mako asked.

"I've been taking some online classes," Bashir said.

Bashir and the pilot talked back and forth.

"He says he can fly the chopper," Bashir said. "He is ex-Venezuelan military. He can take us anywhere we want to go."

"Just what we need," Mako said. "Ask him if he knows anything about the plane."

Bashir continued to talk to the pilot.

"He doesn't," Bashir said. "But he heard these men talking about it. He said they are going to a place in the highlands. I'm not sure what it means. A teepee? It sounds something like that . . ."

The pilot interrupted Bashir.

"Tepui," the man said.

"Tepui?" Bashir asked.

The pilot spoke more to Bashir, and Mako couldn't follow it at all.

"He says the rebels believe the plane crashed on top of one of these tepuis, which are tall flat-topped mountains in the highlands. Part of the rebel group was going there. He doesn't know the exact location. But he says . . ." Bashir said.

Bashir's words were hushed by a gunshot that pinged off the helicopter's frame. It came from behind them.

All three PJs turned at once, laying down suppressing fire in the direction the shooting came from. The pilot kept his head low. More automatic weapons fire came whizzing back at them.

"Bash, get this pilot buddy of yours to spin up this bird. We're getting out of here!" Mako shouted.

◉ CHAPTER 12

Location: Guinea Highlands, Venezuela
Date: June 9th
Time: 0230 hours

Jenkins crept silently through the brush. Up ahead there were at least three men moving through the jungle. They were moving quickly. Glancing over his shoulder, he could see Gage and Garcia behind him. They were properly spaced in a triangle formation. Each of them had a clear field of fire. The problem was that the jungle was so thick, Jenkins could hear the men ahead of him but couldn't see them.

The ground beneath them was gradually rising. In the pre-dawn light, he could see they were at the base of a strange-looking mountain. It must be one of the tepuis he read about in the briefing book. He motioned for Garcia and Gage to join him. He had found a break in the growth where he could finally see the men.

"I think this is one of those tepuis," Jenkins said. "Looks like it's pretty steep. But these guys appear to know their way around. They're taking a trail to the summit," Jenkins stared through his binoculars. He handed them to Garcia, who studied the group ahead of them.

"That's curious," Gage said.

"Why?" Jenkins asked. He already knew the answer, but wanted to know if the young PJ did.

"The way I figure it, they're part of the group that shot the plane down," Gage said. "Some kind of surface-to-air missile that would damage, but not destroy it. They tracked it, or else knew the flight plan. They probably had bad guys all over the area, watching. My guess is the plane went down on top of this mountain."

"That's kind of a stretch," Garcia said.

"Not really," Gage said. "You didn't let me finish. Why else would these guys be hiking up this specific mountain? There are a bunch of other mountains in these highlands. It's a lot of wasted time and effort unless you're sure something's up there."

Garcia was quiet a moment while he thought about it. Then he nodded. "Makes sense. They're a rebel group. They have some access to weapons and funding. But probably not unlimited resources. If there are survivors, I bet they plan to hold them for ransom. Make a big statement," Garcia said.

Jenkins smiled and nodded. "Good work," Jenkins said. "I came to the same conclusion." He pulled his tablet from its pocket on his vest. On the screen was the mountain in front of them.

"Here's what I'm thinking," Jenkins said. "I'll bet you five dollars that one of them is a local. Knows this mountain backwards and forwards. He's going to take them up the easy way."

Jenkins pointed to a spot on the map showing the mountain's west side.

"We're going to go around here," Jenkins said. "And we're going to beat them to the top."

"Five whole dollars?" Garcia said. "I don't know, Loot. Why don't we just take them out now and go get our people?"

"Because one, we're not allowed to just shoot people on sight," Jenkins said. "And two, if we captured them, I'd need somebody to stay behind and guard them. If there are survivors up there, there are going to be injuries. All of us may be needed to provide treatment. We have to try and beat them to the top if we can. Surprise and disarm them and get our people out. If we can't disarm them, well, they won't be able to say they weren't warned." Jenkins stuffed the tablet back in his pocket.

"I still like my plan better," Garcia said.

"Don't worry, we may still use it," Jenkins said. "Let's move out. We're going to go double-time, and we will beat them to the top, understood?"

"Yes, sir!" Garcia and Gage said in unison.

Silently they moved west, gradually angling toward the mountain. They skirted around the group ahead of them. They wanted to keep them in sight, but make sure they weren't spotted. It took them thirty minutes and then they were no longer visible to the rebels.

From reading the briefing book, Jenkins knew that these tepuis dotted the landscape in this part of the Amazon. They were flat at the top, like a mesa, but some of them were close to ten thousand feet high.

Jenkins also knew that they were ghostly and remote. The Venezuelan and Brazilian governments did not often allow access to the mountains. They wanted to preserve their natural state. Because of that, very little was known about them.

PJs operated in all kinds of territory, from the desert to the arctic. They had to be prepared for anything. But these were steep rock walls. They spread out at the base, looking for a way to the top. It would not be easy. Jenkins studied the formation. The climb would be grueling. He was glad he put his squad through regular training.

"Loot," Gage said. "I think I found a spot."

Jenkins and Garcia joined him.

"This will be a tough climb, but it looks doable," Gage said, pointing up to a fissure in the side of the mountain. The rock formation there looked like a stairway was cut into the side of the mountain. "There are natural cutbacks in it. Also looks like someone has worked on it making handholds and steps. Maybe one of the villagers or local tribes made a path up."

"Let's go," Jenkins said.

Jenkins went first with Gage and Garcia behind him. As they climbed, Jenkins thought Gage might be right. It was a mixture of natural and handmade, as if someone carved steps into the rock long ago. It was a steep and difficult climb, but it was getting them to the top.

The sun hadn't come out yet, but it was still incredibly hot and humid. Sweat poured off their faces. About halfway up, they paused to rest. Each man took a long drink from his canteen.

They kept going. As they neared the summit, the climb grew steeper. The steps were narrower. But they were almost there. When they reached a safe spot, Jenkins checked his watch. It had taken them almost two hours to get this far. He hoped they had beat the rebel group to the top.

A few minutes later the ground leveled out. It was rocky. There were far fewer plants than in the jungle below. It was a bit easier to move around and see now.

"All right," Jenkins said. "Let's move out. Gage, I want you to stay at least one hundred yards behind us. At all times. If you can, stay hidden. Have your sniper rifle ready."

"Roger that, lieutenant," Gage said. "What are the rules of engagement?"

"If they're holding hostages, Garcia and I will flank them," Jenkins said. "If they don't surrender peacefully, and you have to, take the shot."

"Yes, sir," Gage said.

Gage waited as Garcia and Lieutenant Jenkins moved from the edge of the tepui toward the center. They were careful, using the rocks and trees they passed by for cover. When they were one hundred yards away, Gage started following them.

On they moved. About a quarter mile in, there were several broken trees limbs in a row littering the ground. It looked like something huge had crashed into them. Something big enough to shear the tops of trees clean off.

Like an airplane.

Another few hundred yards in, smoke was rising into the air. It was obscured by the cloud cover from the ground. They headed towards the smoke. After moving a bit farther, they reached a large natural clearing. There they finally saw the tail section of an aircraft. It looked like a giant had snapped it off the end of a plane and tossed it as far as it could.

At the far end of the clearing was the rest of the wreck. It had come to a stop against a row of trees. The plane had buckled and crumbled in places. The tip of the left wing had broken off. There were two gaping holes in the body of the aircraft.

Behind the aircraft, nearly out of sight, a small group of people were huddled. Some were lying on the ground injured. Others stood with torn and bloody clothes. There were survivors.

Unfortunately, they were being guarded by three men with guns.

"Are you sure he doesn't know which way they were going?" Mako shouted to Bashir over the noise of the chopper.

"No, sergeant, he says they made no mention of it," Bashir said.

"We need a direction," Mako said. "We don't have enough fuel to fly all over the Amazon."

"Well he didn't hear them say anything," Bashir said.

Sergeant George looked at their prisoner. He was a small, wiry man, with shoulder-length dark hair. He refused to give them his name. "Maybe their *amigo* here knows something," Sergeant George said. Mako looked at him.

"That's actually a good idea. Bashir, ask him what he knows," Mako said.

Airman Bashir asked the man a question in

Spanish. The man spat back at him. He cursed and shouted in Spanish.

"I have a feeling he didn't tell us what he knows," Mako said.

"I only understood about half of what he said. Most of it was curse words," Bashir said.

"Huh," Mako said. As the helicopter flew, Bashir was seated across from the prisoner. Mako and Sergeant George were seated on the same bench as the bound man, keeping an eye on the pilot.

"Bashir, switch seats with me," Mako said. They changed positions.

Mako leaned forward until his immense bulk was clearly in the man's space. The captured rebel tried to look brave and defiant. It wasn't easy with this enormous, angry, heavily armed PJ inches from his face. Right then, the man couldn't be sure if Mako was going to ask him a question or toss him out of the chopper.

Mako smiled at the man. It looked like a wolf smiling at a sheep. The man tried very hard to hold Mako's gaze, but he eventually had to look away.

"Airman Bashir," Mako said. "I would like you to explain to this man that he has two options. The first option is to tell us where his comrades are going. Or I can hold him by his ankle outside the chopper. And hope my arm doesn't get tired."

"Uh, sarge?" Bashir said.

"Tell him!" Mako said.

Bashir translated Mako's word to the man. Still defiant, the man sneered at Mako. He let loose a string of curses. Mako inched closer to the man. The prisoner blinked. Mako moved until their noses were almost touching. His size and the look on his face was scary. Mako didn't say anything. He just stared into the prisoner's eyes. The prisoner tried hard to resist. Slowly Mako unlatched the door on the chopper and slid it open. The hot jungle air rushed in. Mako never took his eyes off the man.

Still staring he unbuckled the straps that held the prisoner to the seat. Beads of sweat appeared on the man's forehead. In a few seconds, it was streaming down his face. Finally, he couldn't take it any longer. Fear won. Words poured out of his mouth like a rushing river. Bashir had to tell him to slow down so he could be understood.

Mako slid the door shut and buckled the straps. The man sank back in his seat, visibly relaxed. He stared at Mako as if the big sergeant were some kind of beast.

"What did he say, Bash?" Mako asked.

It took Bashir a moment because both he and Sergeant George were laughing.

"Man, Mako," George said. "For a second, I thought you were going to throw him out of the helicopter."

Mako looked at George. "Who says I wasn't?" Mako said.

"He said his group was headed toward the highlands west of here," Bashir said. "They have information on where the plane crashed. It's on top of a mountain. He doesn't know the exact location. He also thinks you might be insane. I assured him you were. Just to remind him not to try anything funny."

Mako thought for a moment. "West of here, huh? All right, Bashir, tell the pilot to turn us around and find that mountain. Maybe we'll get lucky and get into radio range with Loot," Mako said.

Bashir told the pilot to head west. Nodding, the pilot banked the chopper and turned.

Mako, Bashir, and George readied their

equipment. Mako tried to reach Lieutenant Jenkins on the radio. There was no response.

As the chopper roared through the sky, the three PJs could only imagine what they might be flying into.

Lieutenant Jenkins crouched in the bush. He counted seven captives outside the plane. Three were lying on the ground. They were most likely too injured to stand. Four of them, two men and two women, stood near the others. One of the men standing had his arm in a sling made from a necktie. The other man and the two women had cuts and bruises but didn't look seriously injured. From this distance, it was impossible to tell the extent of the injuries of those on the ground.

"Garcia? Are you in position?" Jenkins whispered into the microphone.

"Roger," Garcia said.

"Gage, do you have overwatch?" Jenkins asked.

"Roger that, sir," Gage said. Overwatch was exactly what it sounded like. Gage was set up as a sniper. He was out of sight. He was watching over them—his eyes glued to the rebels.

Jenkins needed to set up a tactical plan.

He watched the rebels as they interacted with the captives. Two of the men stood guarding the hostages, but also letting their eyes sweep the jungle every few seconds. They were alert. The way they constantly looked around, he wondered if they were expecting trouble.

"Listen up, guys," Jenkins said into the microphone. "The two guards are on extra alert. They might have been warned help was coming. The other guy asking questions is their leader. He matches the description for Miguel Ramos. Also known as La Vibora, the Viper. It would be great if we could take him alive. But not at the expense of the hostages."

Jenkins took one final look through the binoculars. Miguel wasn't getting the answers he wanted. Frustrated, he slapped the man with the back of his hand. Shouting at him, he grabbed one of the women. Turning her so she was in front of him, he threatened her with his weapon. He started screaming again.

"Loot, you seeing this?" Gage came over the radio.

"Roger," Jenkins said. "We go on one. Gage, be ready to take out Ramos first if things go south. Garcia, you have the guard closest to you. I have the other. Garcia and I will go on my count. Three . . . two . . . one. Go!"

Jenkins and Garcia burst out of the underbrush into the clearing.

"Hands up! Hands up!" Jenkins shouted as he and Garcia moved to the cluster of people. "Nobody move! United States Air Force! Drop your weapons."

What happened next happened fast.

Both guards bought their guns around. Jenkins and Garcia fired almost simultaneously. Both men dropped. Neither Jenkins nor Garcia stopped. They trained their weapons on Miguel Ramos, moving toward him.

Miguel looked around, his eyes wild. He had yet to realize what happened. Jenkins and Garcia were rapidly advancing on him. Miguel pulled the woman closer.

"Drop the gun! Drop the gun!" Garcia shouted to him in Spanish.

"Stop! Step back!" Miguel said in English, threatening to harm his hostage.

Jenkins and Garcia kept moving until they were each about ten yards from Ramos. The woman cried as Miguel held her tight.

"Listen to me," Jenkins said. "You've got no way out here. Put down the gun. Right now."

"No. I will die first!" Miguel said.

"Nobody needs to die," Jenkins said.

"Foolish American," Miguel said. "You come into our country. You come with your money and your machines. You bribe our government and brag about it at fancy parties. I will bring freedom and justice to my people!"

"You may be right," Jenkins said. "But we are going to get our people. Put down the gun and leave. Fight your fight for the people another day."

Jenkins had seen this before. Miguel was a fanatic. He was more than willing to die.

Just then, Mako's voice came over the radio. "Loot? It's Mako. We're about ten minutes out. What's the situation?" Jenkins couldn't respond without Ramos hearing him.

"Listen to me, Miguel," Jenkins said. "You're not going to make it out of here."

"Wrong!" Miguel said. "I have more men on the way. You are the ones who will die."

"Negative," Jenkins said. "We've already taken down two of your people. You're the only one left."

Jenkins was trying to feed Mako information while he talked to Ramos.

"Loot," Mako said. "I read you. One bad guy. Likely holding a hostage, I'm guessing. Hang on. We're coming!"

"Listen to reason, Miguel," Jenkins said. "You've got no way out here."

Ramos said nothing but looked around desperately.

"Lieutenant," Gage said over the radio. "I have a shot. Should I take it?"

"Miguel, listen to me!" Jenkins said. "You can't get out of this. I've got a sniper out there. You're right in the middle of his sights. I've got more men inbound. Drop the gun, Miguel."

"You lie, like all Americans!" said Miguel. "I will—"

He never got the chance to finish. The bullet from Gage's sniper rifle made a hissing sound. It hit Miguel in the shoulder, and he spun away to the ground, dropping his gun. Garcia was on him in a heartbeat. The woman he had been holding slumped to the ground.

Jenkins heard the familiar sound. A chopper rose up out of the clouds and circled over the area. It was a welcome sight.

"Here comes the cavalry," Mako said over the radio.

Gage came into the clearing from the bush. Bashir and Mako left the helicopter and rushed to the injured. Sergeant George stayed back to watch the prisoner and the surrounding area. There was a chance the Viper had more people on the way. They wanted no surprises.

Jenkins walked to Miguel. He was awake but in obvious pain. Jenkins searched for weapons.

Miguel stared at Jenkins, still defiant. "Are you going to kill me now, American?" Miguel snarled.

Jenkins knelt beside him. He laid down his rifle and opened his medical kit.

"No," Jenkins said. "I'm going to treat your wounds."

◎ EPILOGUE

After the chopper arrived on the mountaintop, the PJs had treated the injured. The most seriously wounded were the two men lying on the ground at the crash site. One of them was the ambassador. Both men had serious head wounds. The others had broken bones, cuts, and bruises. Two Pave Hawk helicopters came in from the highlands. They evacuated the wounded people.

Three members of the ambassador's staff had not survived the crash. After the Pave Hawks left, a big helicopter called a Jolly arrived to carry away the bodies, the prisoner, and the rest of the PJs. Jenkins and Mako had the pilot fly them to Miguel's compound. While he was being treated, Miguel had pleaded with Jenkins.

"You have won," Miguel said. "Leave me behind to fight for my people. You know the government here."

"Negative," Jenkins said. "You shot down an aircraft carrying a US diplomat. There were casualties. You don't walk away from that."

Miguel was silent while Jenkins treated his shoulder wound. The pain was intense. But Miguel was able to bear it.

"Then I have one request," Miguel said.

Jenkins did not respond.

Miguel continued nonetheless. "Allow me to see my mother before you take me away," he said. "She is dying. I will not see her again."

"Negative," Jenkins said.

"Señor! Please!" said Miguel. "Look at me. I swear to you. She is very ill. The end is near. It may have come already. Please allow me to see her one more time."

Jenkins looked at Miguel. Jenkins had always been good at reading people. Miguel was looking at him, his eyes bright despite the gunshot wound. He did not have the stare of the Viper. He was being truthful.

Jenkins made the decision to grant Miguel's wish.

When Mako heard what Jenkins planned to do, he nearly fainted. When he couldn't talk Jenkins out of it, he insisted on going along. They took the helicopter

Miguel had stolen. The pilot was happy to fly them
to Miguel's compound. Except for his mother and her
nurse, it was deserted. When word of what happened
to the Viper's rebels spread, the remaining members of
the Army of Venom moved to another location.

Inside the compound, Miguel stood beside his
mother's bedside. His hands were bound behind
him. He watched her sleep. Her cheeks were sunken.
Despite the air conditioning, sweat lined her brow.

He leaned over and gently kissed her on the cheek.
She did not move. Her breathing was shallow.

Miguel said a prayer over his mother. He opened
his eyes and looked at Lieutenant Jenkins, who
stood next to Sergeant Mako Marks. "Thank you,
lieutenant," Miguel said. "*Gracias*."

Jenkins nodded.

Mako gave Jenkins and urgent look.

"We have to go," Jenkins said.

"I understand," Miguel said.

Miguel kissed his mother one more time. The
three of them exited the building.

The sun was lowering in the sky. It had been a
very long day. Jenkins was proud of his team. They
had performed splendidly. They knew their jobs. And

with every mission like this they only gained more experience. They got better.

"Now to the extraction point," Jenkins said. "Time to finish out the operation."

"These things we do . . . ," Mako said.

The three men left the compound. The chopper disappeared in the jungle.

GLOSSARY

AMAZON—A large river that runs almost entirely across the South American continent.

AMBASSADOR—A government official who represents their country in a foreign country.

CAT ALPHA—Short for 'Category Alpha'. A category alpha patient is one that is seriously injured and requires immediate medical attention.

EQUATOR—An imaginary line drawn around the earth, equally distant from both poles, dividing the earth into northern and southern hemispheres.

GOLDEN HOUR—When a patient has been wounded or injured, the first hour after the injury happens is the Golden Hour. Patients who can reach a hospital for treatment within the Golden Hour have far better chances of surviving their injury.

PAVE HAWK—The Sikorsky HH-60 helicopter, the primary craft used by PJs.

RAIN FOREST—A type of geography that is mostly thick forest with a large and diverse animal and plant population.

REBELS—People who fight against a government or ruler.

TEPUI—A mesa or flat-topped mountain in parts of Venezuela and Brazil.

INFORMATION BRIEFING:
THE AMAZON

Location: South America

Name History: The river was given its name by Spanish soldiers who were the first Europeans to explore it. Rainforest and River.

The Amazon River is just over 4,300 miles long.

The Tepuis in Venezula are mesas. The name Tepui means "House of the Gods."

Some Tepuis are so high they have their own unique ecosystems.

A MIGHTY ECOSYSTEM

The Amazon rainforest is so large it comprises half the total of all rainforests on the planet. It is estimated that over 10 million animal species live in the Amazon rainforest. The Amazon River carries more water than any river on earth. It runs more than 4,300 miles (nearly 7,000 kilometers) in length, making it slightly shorter than the Nile River. The soldiers claimed to have fought battles against hordes of female warriors on the shores of the river. They thought these fighters must be the Amazons of Greek mythology, a fierce tribe of women warriors.

ABOUT THE AUTHOR

Michael P. Spradlin is the *New York Times* bestselling author of more than thirty books for children and adults. His books include the international bestselling trilogy *The Youngest Templar*, the Edgar nominated *Spy Goddess* series and the Wrangler Award Winning *Off Like the Wind: The First Ride of the Pony Express*. He lives in Lapeer, Michigan. Visit his website at www.michaelspradlin.com.

ABOUT THE ILLUSTRATOR

Spiros Karkavelas is a concept artist and photographer based in Greece. He graduated from Feng Zhu School of Design in Singapore in 2013 and has done work with various video game and book publishing companies. His realistic illustrations often have a theme of modern-day or futuristic warfare, and he draws inspiration from true war stories, the realities of the battlefield, and how war brings out both the worst and best in human nature.

DISCUSSION QUESTIONS

1. The PJs have to be prepared for incredibly dangerous situations, from diving out of planes or sneaking through jungles. Discuss what you think the most difficult part of their mission was. Why?

2. The PJs mission doesn't go xactly to plan with the US ambassador's capture by Miguel's soldiers on top of the tepuis. How do you think the PJs carry on when their operation seems impossible?

3. The Viper caused a lot of damage and many were hurt in his mission. Discuss why you think the PJs let him see his mother one last time?

WRITING PROMPTS

1. Viper Strike takes places among the Tepuis in Venezuela. Think of another place with unique geography like Venezuela. Write up a mission plan that sends the PJs to this place.

2. In Viper Strike, the PJs must parachute into Venezuela. Imagine you are a PJ on a mission and when you jump your parachute doesn't open. Write what happens next.

3. Snakes, alligators, and jaguars are just a few of the animals in the Amazon rain forest. Write a story where the PJs encounter one of these animals on a mission.